SPF CA

THE GREENHORN Diary

AN ADVENTURE STORY

Illustrated by Moa Rosenberg

AMHERST PUBLISHING

This novella is dedicated to every person who has suffered the physical, mental and emotional anguish of carrying shame with them throughout their lifetime, whether or not they know and understand its origin.

AUTHOR'S NOTE

The Greenhorn Diary is one of a series of adventure stories involving growing up in a family on the edge of the wilderness of northern Minnesota. The series is intended to capture the coming-of-age wonderment brought on by experiencing the natural world as viewed from the perspective of a brotherhood. Readers are advised that this adventure story includes content that may not be appropriate for children under the age of 12.

"**Green·horn** *n* [obs. *greenhorn* (animal with young horns)] (1682) 1 : an inexperienced or unsophisticated person 2 : a newcomer (as to a country) unacquainted with local manners and customs."

- *Webster's Ninth New Collegiate Dictionary (Copyright 1986 by Merriam Webster Inc.)*

"If what Billy Pilgrim learned from the Tralfamadorians is true, that we will all live forever, no matter how dead we may sometimes seem to be, I am not overjoyed. Still – if I am going to spend eternity visiting this moment and that, I'm grateful that so many of those moments are nice."

- Kurt Vonnegut, Jr., '*Slaughterhouse-Five, or The Children's Crusade: A Duty-Dance with Death*' (1969)

THE LATE-AUTUMN sun was rising over the lake as they drove down the gravel road running along its meandering shore. Turning into the driveway covered by a scattering of wind-blown leaves, they saw the rustic cottage his brother called home. The roof and siding were different shades of worn, cedar shake shingles. They gave the cottage a warm feel, together with the massive stone chimney running up its side. A season's worth of split firewood was neatly stacked to either side of the chimney along the outer wall. For the first time in more than thirty years, it would not be needed this coming winter.

Jonathan, a grey-haired man in his late fifties, drove their sedan up the driveway and parked just beside the entrance. He shut off the engine and then paused for a moment, staring blankly at the cottage without unlocking the car doors.

"You can do this," his wife Harini said. She was younger than her husband and had long, black hair and coffee-colored skin that gave away her Indian heritage. She somehow managed to feel at home in Minneapolis, a good eight hour drive to the south, despite being raised in New York City.

"I'm sure I can manage, Harini. I don't know how I'm going to feel about anything after what happened but I'm pretty sure it's going to be rather painful."

"Just let go of all that," Harini said, placing her hand reassuringly on his shoulder.

"The image of him floating in the freezing water when they found him just keeps reappearing in my mind. I can't make it stop as much as I want to. It just gets more gruesome the harder I try not to think about it."

"Maybe we need to try to stop and approach this whole experience in a different way."

"What is there to think differently about? He's gone and it feels like someone is trying to squeeze my chest until I can't breathe anymore."

"Just take a few deep breaths and try not be so morbid. All I'm suggesting is that we try to focus on all the positives of his life and do our best to forget the end of it. It's just an ending after all, not his life itself."

"It's hard to forget when you're talking about your brother's life. I keep telling myself not be sad and to focus on all the happy times we had together. I know Robbie would think that way in a very literal sense. He had some slightly twisted ideas about time. I know they influenced how he thought about everything, even death."

"My grandmother, Aachi used to tell me stories when I was growing up about India. She lived with us in our apartment on Manhattan after my grandfather died. I spent so much time sitting on Aachi's lap, with my head cuddled into her soft, warm arms. Not long before she died, I remember she told me about the concept of 'kala' in Hinduism."

"Why would you remember that?"

"I have long since forgotten so many of the gods and goddesses Aachi told me stories about but I do remember very well what she told me about *kala.*"

"What is that and why do you think it has anything to do with Robbie's life?"

"Aachi was taught that basically the same concept applies to both time and death. The god of death, Yama, determines how long a person's supposed to live on Earth. He is the manifestation of time. Once human life is over, time relative to that human being ceases to exist and becomes eternal, without any beginning or ending."

"I can assure you that's not how Robbie thought about time. It had more to do with *Tralfamadorians.*"

"What religion is that?"

"It's not a religion at all. It was just a different way of looking at time he got from a book he read. I think it affected his whole life. If you asked Robbie, he would've told you he's not really gone. That's just the way he thought about time."

"I never thought he was that spiritual."

"It was slightly more scientific than spiritual, or maybe just plain weird sums it up best. He thought about time and space in a crazy four-dimensional reality, one a person could always see and supposedly control but never change."

"In what way?"

"He really thought time was a variable just like three-dimensional space but not in the strict scientific sense of relativity. It was way more random than all that."

"Who can honestly say for certain they know anything about time and space," Harini said.

"Or death and existence for that matter," Jonathan added.

"On a very human level, I just think it is sad that he never married and never seemed to even want any children of his own. I could never understand that about Robbie, like so much else about his life. I can't imagine what our lives would be like now without our two boys. I know he loved his nephews even if he didn't see them very much."

"Some people just choose to go through life alone I guess."

"I'm sure that's right," Harini said. "Are you ready?"

"Whether I am or not, we need to go inside eventually," Jonathan said, opening the car door and stepping out into the crisp autumn air.

They walked up to the heavy wooden front door of the cottage, sheltered by a small pitched roof. Jonathan fumbled with a large set of keys he had been given to find the one that fit. After a few attempts, a rusty-brown, skeleton key eventually unlocked the door. He pushed it open and then held it to permit Harini to step inside first. The pleasant smell of a thousand fires greeted them, absorbed into the woodwork of the cottage. It was tidy and well-kept, as if the occupant had simply decided to go out for a walk and would be back at any moment.

The wooden floor creaked as they stepped into a large living room that ran the length of the cottage, with a picture window looking out over the lake at the far end. In front of a rustic, stone fireplace and hearth was a winged back chair turned towards the window. Along the wall between the fireplace and picture window was a large walnut desk, with drawers running down either side, and large built in books shelves that covered the remaining walls. The desk was covered with papers and binders in neat stacks.

"What's this?" Harini asked, pointing to a large manila envelope that was resting prominently on the desk against a lamp. On the envelope in black, magic-marker letters was written simply '*Johnny*'.

"I don't know. Let me take a look at it." He picked up the envelope and examined it closely. "I don't understand."

"I presume he wanted you, *and only you*, to open it," Harini said after a moment.

Jonathan turned the envelope over in his hands searching for something more. "We've always kept his Will for him, so it can't be that."

"Maybe he wanted to change something in it?"

"If he did, he would have told me. I'm sure it's not that."

"Just open it, dear. You don't have to tell me what's in it if you don't want to." .

"Don't be daft. We're in this together. I don't want to be carrying around secrets for the rest of my life. I've got enough anxiety already."

6

"He was your brother and I don't want to interfere."

"You're not interfering. I'm glad you're here."

"I'm not so sure your brother would be."

"Why would you ever think that? Don't be silly. I'm not sure I could handle this alone right now. I'm just going to open it. I'm sure that's what Robbie wanted us to do."

"So you still think he planned this, don't' you?"

"I'm not saying he did or didn't. I just don't know."

"Maybe this will help."

"Only one way to find out."

Jonathan carefully opened the envelope with a letter opener he had found in a brass cup filled to overflowing with pens and pencils of every shape and size. Once opened, he reached inside and pulled out a paper notebook, yellowed with age and with the year '*1976*' imprinted on the cardstock cover. On the first page was written '*The Greenhorn Diary, by Robert Ericson*' in copperplate handwriting.

"I remember Robbie always loved his calligraphy," he said.

"What do you think it is?"

"It's some sort of diary from 1976."

"Have you seen it before?"

"No, I haven't," he said, thumbing through the diary slowly.

"Not surprising. That was over forty years ago," Harini said as Jonathan continued to thumb through the diary.

"Wait a second! I don't believe this," Jonathan said. "I know exactly what this is now."

"How could you?"

"There are some things from childhood you just don't forget, especially when you had a brother like Robbie. This isn't even supposed to exist."

"Why?"

"Because he said he didn't write it."

"I'm not following you," Harini said. "What didn't he write?"

"This diary. He was supposed to write it and he told his teacher he didn't when we got back from deer hunting. I think her name was Sister Gilbert if I remember correctly. She was my teacher a few years before and I remember she was pretty good looking, sort of like Julie Andrews in '*The Sound of Music*' if you know what I mean. She had a well-earned reputation for being a strict disciplinarian and was infamous for the power she could generate swatting with her wooden ruler."

"That's sounds a bit harsh. Didn't she get in trouble for that?"

"Not in those days. Besides, most of us deserved it anyway. We used to joke about it when we were playing baseball. '*Give it a Sister Gilbert!*' and that sort of thing. Brings back a lot of memories. I'm sure Robbie got a good swat from her when he didn't turn this in."

"Why wouldn't he turn it in?"

"I don't know," Jonathan said, continuing to earnestly flip through the pages. "I can see he spent a long time on it and, if you know Robbie, that means he put a great deal of thought into it."

"I suppose he did end up doing what he loved, right? Maybe that's why he never married or wanted a family."

"I think that's what Philip Larkin's mother told him and I know Robbie was a big fan of his."

"The poet?"

"Yes. They found a letter his mother wrote to him that said if he wanted to dedicate himself fully to writing, a family would take away Larkin's edge and rob him of his gift."

"Didn't he have a really dark side?"

"He sure did – he's the guy who wrote '*Man hands misery to man. It deepens like a coastal shelf. Get out as early as you can, and don't have any kids yourself*'."

"Robbie didn't seem to think that way at all," Harini said, shaking her head. "He always loved playing with the kids and he was certainly handsome and nice enough."

"I can assure Robbie did have his own dark side," Jonathan said. "He was just better at hiding it than most people."

"I know he suffered through a lot of depression. Is that what you're referring to?"

"There was always that. He called it the '*black dog*' when it was there. I was thinking more about something he said to me a long time ago, before things got much worse."

"What did he say?"

"He just said to me more or less out of the blue - 'I know how this ends'."

"What was he referring to?"

"I believe he was actually referring to his life."

"Did he tell you how?"

"Not really, but I know what he said had something to do with his way of thinking about time. It was more metaphysical than anything else. He never said exactly how or why he knew how his life would end but I do believe he genuinely thought he did."

"You never told me that before," Harini said.

"There's a lot about Robbie I'll never understand. Sometimes it's hard to even talk about it."

"I do know he was always terribly shy around people, almost to a fault. It was like he carried damage somewhere way deep inside himself," Harini said.

"I doubt we'll ever know why he was like that," Jonathan said, now staring at the cover of the diary. "I'd sure like to find out, though. Perhaps reading this might give us a few clues," he said. "I'd really like to read it now."

"Right now?"

"Yes, if you don't mind."

"You go right ahead," Harini said, smiling. Why don't you start a fire and go sit in Robbie's chair. I'll fix us some lunch and we can talk about it later."

"Thanks. I think I just need some time with him alone. I knew this was going to be hard but now I'm really looking forward to being with him again, even if it's only through his writing."

"Remember what we talked about in the car. Let's focus on all the happiness and goodness, and not fixate about the way it ended, okay?"

"I swear – I'll do my best."

He walked over to the stone fireplace and immediately recognized a familiar photo on the mantel of himself with Harini and their their two boys. Next to that was a family deer hunting photo that Robbie had framed. It had Robbie and Jonathan in it, together with their father and older brother Paul. They were standing in front of a buck Robbie had shot years ago. Robbie was in the center of the photo with a proud smile on his face as he held up the deer's head by its antlers.

Jonathan grabbed a few logs from the copper basin beside the fireplace, lit the fire and then settled into the wing back chair.

"Here you are," Harini said, walking over to the chair and handing Jonathan a cup of tea.

"Thanks."

"What are you smiling about?"

"I just can't help thinking Robbie planned that everything would end up just like it is now, right down to the firewood," Jonathan said, putting on his reading glasses.

"Knowing Robbie, he probably did," Harini said. "He certainly had a tendency to think too much. Then again, so does his brother."

He smiled again at Harini, opened up the diary and travelled back in time to 1976.

* * *

"The Greenhorn Diary

I actually came up with that name myself believe it or not. You probably already know this but a greenhorn is basically someone who doesn't know anything about something 'cause it's their first time doing it. That pretty much describes me deer hunting.

The only reason I am writing this stupid diary is on account of my 7ᵗʰ grade teacher Sister Gilbert. She is super strict and always seems mad at me even though she tells me I am a good writer. She said I had to write a diary if I was going to miss a week of school to go deer hunting.

My Dad would've taken me out of school anyway no matter what Sister Gilbert said. He told me that going out hunting in the woods teaches kids more than anything they're gonna learn in the 7ᵗʰ grade. I decided to make Sister Gilbert happy anyway and not cause any trouble. After all, the only thing I had to do was write down the stuff that happened each day and turn it in. I didn't bother telling my Dad about the assignment or what a big deal Sister Gilbert was making about me being out of school for a week.

Anyhow, I plan to write this diary to record everything that happens as truthfully as possible. I'm going to be honest even if it means I have to cross out loads of things that Sister Gilbert can't read or anyone else for that matter. I like writing things down so I can remember them and I am sure I'm not going to want to forget anything about my first time deer hunting. I've been looking forward to this for so long now that it's hard to believe the day will finally arrive tomorrow when it's going to happen in true life. I know if I were a Tralfamadorian, it is going to be a day I am going to spend a lot of time looking at over and over again! <u>Note to self</u>: try to avoid time travel . You're just going to have to cross it all out anyway.

The Greenhorn Diary

Day 1 - Saturday, November 6, 1976

Actually, I should probably say this is Day 2 on account of us spending Friday setting up camp. That was as much fun as anything I've ever done even if it was hard work. We drove up into the big woods by Beltrami State Forest in Minnesota and went to our campsite. We don't actually own the land. Dad says the State does because it's way too wet and cold to be used by anyone but nature. All the other hunters know we camp there so they don't bother us. It is almost like we have a legal right to be there and hunt although I know it isn't written down anywhere. Dad says it doesn't have a legal basis. It's just hunting tradition and it is more or less respected by most people that hunt up here.

Anyway, yesterday we drove in and set up the pop-up camper and a tent outside for our supplies and hunting gear. We had to dig a hole for the camp toilet. Dad brought along a toilet seat so it feels sort of like a normal toilet except you're freezing when you finally sit there. I did it first thing this morning before anyone else and I thought my butt was going to actually get frozen to the seat. I vowed that if I have to go tomorrow, I'm going to wait it out until somebody goes first. I think Johnny knew that because he used the toilet just about as soon as I managed to stand up and pull up my pants. To tell you the truth, I actually thought it was majestic sitting there out in nature. When I told that to Johnny later, he joked that it should be since you're sitting on a 'throne'. Anyway, it sure beats our bathroom back home where you sit staring at the bathtub.

The camper itself has a toilet but we're not supposed to use it cause it's not properly hooked up to anything. The camper also has a table where four people can sit down and eat or play cards. It even has a gas stove and gas heating. Everything folds away and it is easy to sleep all four of us without any trouble. I can't imagine a cooler place to be on this Earth! Dad says we're spoiled because we have it so comfy. If you believe his stories, he more or less slept out in a tent on the bare ground when he was a kid back in Michigan hunting with my grandfather.

Anyhow, today was the opening day of deer hunting. It's what I would call the premier day because it's the day you are supposedly the most likely to shoot a buck. I was so excited when I woke up and realized it was actually happening. I have been counting down the days since school started and reading loads of books about hunting and survival in the wilderness. My Mom never liked hunting that much and she gave me a different book to read. I'm glad I read it but, man, it sure has made me think more than I probably should about time and such - 'so it goes.'

This morning didn't turn out particularly well but I tried to look on the bright side. Mom always said you'll find one if you just look hard enough and I assure you it took a great deal of looking today! Dad stayed back with me at camp and we walked down a trail only about 200 yards from camp and found a tall tree that looked out over a large clearing in the woods. I unloaded my shotgun with slugs to be safe and then Dad helped me get started climbing the tree. He insisted that I climb as high as I possibly could all the way into the upper branches. I was about 30 feet up the tree when the rope I had tied to my shotgun slipped off my shoulder. The shotgun fell down and bounced off a couple of branches before hitting the ground right next to my Dad.

I looked down and saw that my shotgun was in two pieces. It's one of those moments I'm pretty sure I'm going to be hopping over time-wise in the future. I called down to my Dad as quietly as possible, 'What now?' He responded, 'You need to come down, Son.' I guess that was pretty obvious given I couldn't shoot anything without my shotgun. I climbed down the tree and we walked back down the trail to camp together. I might have been crying a little bit but I don't think it was too obvious. I tried my best to hide it because I didn't want my Dad to think I was a big baby.

When we got back to camp, Dad used some electrical tape to try to hold the stock of the shotgun together. I'm not talking about a little electric tape but layer after layer, crisscrossing this way and that right up to the trigger guard. Still, I don't think he was comfortable having me use it. In the end, he gave me the family's sawed-off 20 gauge shotgun to use instead. My brother had been duck hunting and got the barrel plugged crawling along a muddy ditch. When he fired it, the barrel exploded a few inches behind the front sights. Dad said he was lucky he didn't get killed. We were able to saw off the barrel and still have it just long enough to be a legal length. The shot pattern was really big so it was good for rabbits and grouse. No one really knew whether it would work with a heavy slug rather than pellets. Dad told me it should be accurate for at least 50 yards or so. Any farther than that would be pushing it. It was safer than using the 16 gauge taped together which might have exploded when I fired it. That wouldn't have made for the greatest ending to my first deer hunting trip, or time in general for that matter.

This afternoon, Dad went hunting off in a section of the woods a mile or so away. The deer population is supposedly better there and it's where he and my older brothers have shot lots of deer before. He let me go off on my own provided I stayed around camp. I went down the trail to the clearing we had been at that morning and then just sort of wandered around quietly. I didn't see any deer but I did find something incredible. In a meadow just off the main clearing was a buck rut. I don't know if Sister Gilbert even knows what that is but it's basically a scrape in the ground a buck makes to mark his territory. That way the does know where to find him. It usually means he's gonna come back there soon if he wants a girlfriend! What was even better was that I found an oak tree that looked over the meadow. It was so easy to climb, especially considering the tree I had to shimmy up this morning. The tree was also situated perfectly so that I could watch out over the meadow.

Unfortunately, it was starting to get dark by the time I found the tree so I had to walk back to camp. I didn't have any trouble finding the trail and I even used my compass to make sure I was heading in the right direction. At least, I had found the bright side about the day Mom always wanted me to find. I now have a gun that sort of works and a great place to go hunting tomorrow. For the rest of my life, that will be what happened the premier day I went deer hunting. If I'm honest, I'll probably hop over a lot of that day time-wise when I'm searching for the happiest moments.

Day 2 - Sunday, November 7, 1976

I was so excited when I woke up this morning on account of the buck rut. I even dreamt about him showing up in the meadow, huge antlers and all. In my dream, I couldn't actually shoot him because he was so awesome. But it was just a dream and all. Anyhow, I was really determined to sit up in that oak tree all day if necessary until he showed up again. Then I wouldn't get teased like I did last night by my brothers about dropping my shotgun and breaking it in two. I couldn't actually wait to go to sleep even though I liked playing cards. To tell you the truth, I didn't really mind too much them making fun of me. After all, I guess I deserved it and the teasing made me feel like I belonged.

My Dad said this was one of the warmest years we've ever had hunting. I've heard stories of people trying to hunt in minus 30 degrees and that doesn't sound like too much fun. It was just below freezing during the daytime. That was cold enough so the snow wouldn't melt totally but warm enough so you could stay in your post without having to get down and walk around to get warm. And that's exactly what I did. Dad let me go on my own after I told him where the oak tree was located. He knew about it already and said he probably should have put me in that tree opening morning on account of it not being so high and easy to climb.

Anyhow, I found the tree after hunting around a little bit in the early morning light. By 7:00 am I was already up in the tree and ready for anything. The only problem with this tree was that there wasn't exactly a good place to sit. The best place I could find that would allow me to take a shot out over the meadow was a thick branch that angled upward something like 45 degrees. If I sat on that branch facing the tree trunk with my legs to either side of it I could just about get my boots onto two branches below me. To do that I almost had to stand on the balls of my feet. If I relaxed my feet, it pushed my crotch into the tree in a way that was pretty uncomfortable.

I didn't hear a sound hardly that whole morning except a squirrel hopping around by the base of my tree and a grouse that was in some brush along the meadow. Then just before noon I heard a car pull in to the camp. That's how close I was to camp actually. I heard lots of excited voices that I recognized as my two brothers. One of them had clearly shot a deer by how excited they sounded. I had already been up in my tree for more than five hours so I decided to climb down and hurry back to camp to see for myself.

Turns out it was my Dad who shot the deer. It was what we call a forked buck, usually a deer that's in its second year. I don't know how to describe it but when you are in a camp together, it feels like everyone shot it together. We were all so happy. When Dad field dressed it (basically taking out the insides), he saved the heart which our family traditionally ate in the evening fried with a bit flour and salt and pepper. We all worked together to hang up the deer and then went in for some lunch.

That afternoon, I went out again to the oak tree. I spent the time there until just before dark thinking about that deer and the one I might get if I was patient and quiet enough. The tree was great and all but it was really uncomfortable the way I described before. I tried to find some other position but the one I mentioned was the only one that seemed to work. Walking back to camp, I felt as determined as ever and really hopeful that tomorrow would be the day that big buck returned to its rut. Then people would be congratulating me for a change.

Day 3 - Monday, November 8, 1976

I don't even know where to start to describe today. I was out early because I knew that buck would have to check the rut it made at least every three days if it wanted a girlfriend. I sure didn't want to miss it. I was up in the oak tree by 7:00 am again and ready for anything. The light snow cover was still holding so I vowed I was going to check for any deer tracks before going in for lunch if I didn't see anything this morning.

Well, guess what - I did! It was just before 8:00 am and I was daydreaming and trying to stop my legs from falling asleep by shifting my weight from one side to the other. Then I suddenly heard the brush crunch behind me. I knew it wasn't a squirrel because it would've been the biggest squirrel in history. The only problem was that the sound came from the exact opposite direction I was facing. I slowly turned my head around until I thought it would almost twist off. I could just see the outline of a deer moving through the underbrush towards me but I couldn't see whether it was a doe or a buck. My heart started racing like a madman.

The problem was that I had absolutely no way to turn and shoot in that direction unless I literally moved down to the lower branches and that meant making a lot of noise. I decided the best thing was just to sit and wait and let it get closer. With each crunching step closer my heart pounded harder until I thought I was literally gonna pass out and fall out of the tree. I couldn't keep my head turned around the whole time because it hurt just to turn enough to be able to see it. When the deer was no more than 20 yards from the tree, it stepped out of the brush and into a small clearing and I got my first good look at it. You probably guessed already but it was a doe.

I desperately wanted it to be a buck but she was so beautiful. She might've smelled me as she got closer 'cause she was downwind and I hadn't taken a bath in four days. Heck, I could probably even smell myself then. She turned to the north and walked slowly through the meadow where I could look at her without spraining my neck. I watched her slowly walk over towards the buck rut at the end of the meadow. She still had her tail down so she couldn't have been too alarmed. Before she made it across the meadow though, she suddenly leaped to the east and into the brush again. I'm not sure what startled her but wow did she jump high. I think the word I would use to describe her would be majestic. Then again, I already used that to describe the feeling of sitting on the toilet so I better just say it was regal, which I think means about the same thing.

I didn't see anything else the rest of the morning other than the red squirrel who clearly lived in the pine tree just to the east of the meadow. I had watched him so many times I even gave him the name 'Old Red'.

Watching him jump around was at least a distraction because, I have to admit, when you don't hear or see anything, it can actually get kind of boring sitting in a tree with your legs falling asleep and your butt getting sore or your crotch getting pushed into a tree trunk. I kept on thinking about that stupid book Mom gave me and wondering whether time was really like that. The more I thought about it, the more confusing everything seemed to get.

Anyhow, I checked the meadow before heading in for lunch and saw the tracks where the doe had been but nothing else. I was beginning to wonder if maybe somebody already shot the buck that made the rut. If so, I was probably just wasting my time. But my Dad said patience is the greatest weapon a hunter will ever have and I'm sure he's right. He should be. After all, he's been deer hunting for 30 years.

I told everybody about the doe while we ate some soup and cold sandwiches. My brothers kept on kidding me that I was just making things up. They also thought I wasn't really hunting on account of I was just going and sitting in the same old tree all the time without exploring the woods for more sign. I

26

told them I was going to watch that buck rut all week if that was what it takes. I can be pretty determined when I want to be. They just laughed at me the way brothers do sometimes.

That afternoon, my oldest brother Paul shot a buck just before dark and we all went to drag it in. It was a big ten pointer and he was so proud of himself. I was too. It was a big deer and we had to drag it a long way through some heavy brush. That's the great thing about deer camp. You feel like you're all in it together. We have two deer now and still two more deer tags to fill. I sure hope one of those tags goes on my buck!

* * *

A nun in formal habit stood beside her modest, wooden desk at the front of the small classroom. The freshly-cleaned blackboard behind her made her features appear radiant, especially given the starched, white guimpe she wore around her face and shoulders. With a book in one hand and a wooden yardstick in the other, she commanded the attention of her 14 students. Her yardstick served primarily as a pointer although her students knew it had a variety of purposes. It was only October and she was already on her third one.

They sat quietly at their student desks at full attention awaiting her next instructions. Their desks had a wooden top that opened up to store possessions, and an attached chair. Over the past few years, the desks and connected chairs had become proportionately smaller compared to the students who occupied them. They were all between the ages of 12 and 13 and were almost as close as siblings, having spent the past so many years in a single classroom and playing together on the school's small playground. This was to be there last year together before leaving for the much larger public school.

Robbie sat in the row of desks farthest from the blackboard. It was the ideal position to make it into the cloakroom at the back of the class and and then be the first one out the door at recess. On his desk, he held open a mathematics work book, propped at a 45 degree angle away from Sister Gilbert. Inside of that, he had hidden the smaller book he was actually reading. He was startled when he heard Sister Gilbert call his name loudly for what was apparently the second time.

"Yes, Sister," he said, quickly looking up at her. By now, the blackboard had a number of equations written on it. "I'm sorry, Sister – what was the question again?"

"I already asked you it twice and I'm not going to repeat it again," she said, walking over towards his desk. As she approached, Robbie tried to slip the book he was reading into the compartment in his desk as nonchalantly as possible.

"What is that?"

"What is what?" Robbie said, staring up at her.

"Don't you be clever with me, young man. What did you just put in your desk?"

"Nothing at all, Sister."

"Open your desk."

"It has all my stuff in it."

"I don't care! Open it this instant," Sister Gilbert said, raising her voice to a level all of her students immediately recognize as a final warning.

"It was just another book," Robbie said.

"Hand it over right now!" All the students watched as Sister Gilbert brought down her ruler with a loud "thwack!" on Robbie's desk. He immediately opened it and pulled out the book, handing it to her timidly. She took a quick look at the cover and shook her head.

"You should not be reading this sort of thing. Not at your age and especially not in the middle of our mathematics class."

"I'm sorry, Sister."

"You should be apologizing to all of your classmates as well for disrupting their learning. I want to see you after school today."

"Yes, Sister," Robbie said in a voice so quiet it could hardly be heard.

"You should be very ashamed of yourself, Robert Ericson!" Sister Gilbert said in a stern voice. After glaring at him for a moment, she turned and walked back to the front of the class. She placed the confiscated book face down on her desk and continued on with her lesson.

The next time Sister Gilbert turned to face the blackboard again, most of the students quickly turned their heads to cast a quick glance at Robbie with faces showing various degrees of disdain. The only reassuring smile came from Elton, his closest friend whose desk was in the row right next to Robbie's. Elton, was thin and lanky with coke-bottle glasses and the sort of curly blond hair that stuck up like he had just come out of a wind-tunnel. He was an only-child and lived a few houses down on the same gravel road as Robbie. They usually walked home from school together.

When the math lesson finally ended, Sister Gilbert made a rather unusual announcement to the class. She said the boys would be going out to recess by themselves and the girls would be staying behind. This was met with triumphant whoops and cheers from the boys, who had been taken totally by surprise. The girls, on the other hand, sat with knowing smiles on their faces. They seemed to already be aware of what was going on and had somehow managed not to tell any of the boys as if sworn to secrecy.

Once outside, Elton and Robbie leaned against a brick wall watching the other boys playing marbles on the pavement. Marbles had become the go-to game earlier that fall and all the other boys had their own small collections. Most of the games were played *'for keeps'* or simply *'keepsies'*, meaning the winner retained his vanquished opponent's marble. Of course, that didn't mean the student with the most marbles was the best player; it just meant his parents were the most indulgent or that he had been given or (slightly more likely) successfully stolen a large collection from an older brother.

When the marble craze first hit, everyone was mostly overcome by the aesthetics of the various sizes, colors and designs of the marbles. Words like *'shooters'*, *'cat's eye'*, *'piries'*, *'clearies'*, *'crockies'* and, the most feared, *'steelies'* were bandied about the playground as if common English. Their games had become purely about amassing the highest valued collection, with each different type of marble possessing its own tacitly agreed value among the players. Like all such fads hitting the school, marbles would be forgotten in a few months and no one would mention them again, let alone bring their collection in to the school.

Robbie and Elton were the only boys who didn't have a marble collection. They had played a few times when the craze first hit but then one of the bigger boys named Larry challenged Elton to play a game of *keepsies* in front of all the other boys. Without much choice, Elton agreed but also asked him if they could play '*quitsies*', as well. This meant a player could quit the game at any time, ensuring he didn't lose his marble. Since Elton only had one marble, he thought it seemed like a reasonable request. The other boys considered *quitsies* to be a cowards way out and teased Elton about it mercilessly. After that, his nickname became "*Quitsies*" whenever they were out of earshot of Sister Gilbert.

"Bunch of lemmings," Robbie said, leaning his head back against the cold bricks. "Do you think they even wonder why we're outside and the girls aren't?"

"I'm not sure. I think the guys are mostly happy to just get to play without the girls getting in the way. Lately, the girls always seem to want to come over and be annoying all the time. It's not like any of them want to play marbles. They just seem to want the boys' attention. At least some of them, anyway. They never used to be like that," Elton said.

"It is a lot different this year. Everyone used to play together at recess. Can you think of a single girl who plays marbles now?" Robbie asked.

"What about JoAnne?"

"Yes, but she's a tomboy. All the other girls could care less."

"I guess you're right," Elton said, after a moment.

"What do you suppose the girls are really talking about in there? It's really bothering me."

"I have no idea but I bet it has something to do with *sex*," Elton said, whispering the last word.

"Why do you think that?"

"Why else would they only want to speak to the girls. If you didn't notice, some of them are really starting to look different," Elton said, poking Robbie in the ribs with his elbow.

"Stop it – I know what you mean. Do you remember how Marcia looked last year?"

"Yeah, you wouldn't know if she had her sweater on frontwards or backwards. Lately, I'm pretty sure she's even *wearing a bra*." Once again, Elton's voice had gone down to a whisper.

"I noticed that too. I think lots of the girls are wearing them now," Robbie said.

"That's why I think they're talking about sex. What else could it be about?"

"I don't think you need to whisper," Robbie said. "I'm sure nobody can hear you."

"I wonder when they're going to keep us inside and give us a talking to and make the girls go outside instead," Elton said.

"I don't remember my older brothers ever telling me anything about that," Robbie said.

"Why don't you ask them? I would if I had an older brother. You've got two for cripes' sake."

"You've gotta be kidding. I could never ask them about something like that," Robbie said.

"Not even Johnny?"

"I'm pretty sure either one of them wouldn't stop teasing me 'til the day I die."

After a while, Robbie and Elton noticed the other boys had finished their games of marbles and were now staring over at them. The biggest one, who also had the largest marble collection by far, started walking over towards them.

"Hey Quitsies," he yelled. "Care for a game of marble."

"I'm quite certain it's called 'marbles', Larry," Elton said in a nervous manner.

"Not when you've only got one of them like you, Quitsies!" he responded, laughing loudly.

The other boys behind him started laughing as well, only far too loudly to be genuine.

"Leave him alone you diminutive, intellectually-challenged primate," Robbie said in a calm voice.

"What'd you call me?" the boy responded, turning menacingly towards him.

"Look each word up yourself. You might even learn something."

"I don't happen to have a dictionary with me right now," the boy said, poking Robbie in the chest.

"How surprising. When you get around to it, you'll find I just called you a *'little stupid monkey'* if you must know."

The boy grabbed Robbie by his jacket collar and almost lifted him off his feet against the wall. "You're lucky you have your older brother, otherwise you would be drinking your food through a straw for the next month."

"You'll be lucky if I don't tell him what you just did or you'll be the one using a straw. Let go of me right now."

The boy put Robbie down on his feet again. "One of these days, Robbie. You're gonna be mighty sorry," he said. As he let go of Robbie, they heard the door to the playground open and then the bell ringing loudly to end recess.

As they hurriedly walked inside, Elton whispered to Robbie, "I sure wish I had an older brother like you."

"I can guarantee it's not all good, Elton."

"I'm sure it's not, but still…"

* * *

Day 4 - Tuesday, November 9, 1976

Last night we played cards later than usual. We were all happy that we got another deer and no one seemed to be able to win the card game we were playing. I could tell Dad and Paul were pretty tipsy. We laughed a lot but we ended up not getting to bed until way too late given we usually get up at 5:30 am each morning. So when I woke up this morning, I just wanted to stay in my sleeping bag. It was the first time I felt like that since we've been at deer camp. I didn't make it out to my tree until just after 7:30 am. It might have even been a bit later than that in actual fact but I didn't want to check my watch.

I didn't hear a thing all morning except for Old Red and Pretty Girl. That's the name I've given to the grouse that keeps on hopping around behind me. Like I said before, it's better than not hearing anything. Otherwise it's too easy to start thinking about time and space and all that. I shouldn't blame the book Mom gave me because the problem actually started when I read this book called 'Jonathan Livingston Seagull'. That book can basically make you wonder whether time and space are just an illusion. I kept thinking that if that's really true about time and space, then I really wouldn't mind that stupid buck showing up right here and right now!

Anyhow, he didn't. The afternoon post was more of the same. Without any wind, even the slightest sound in the woods registers. When I tried not to think about time and space, I ended up thinking about that doe I saw yesterday. How can nature be so weird that a doe wastes so much energy just to get pregnant and have a fawn or two each year. And the bucks are even worse. They fight, sometimes to the death, just to be the one that gets to be with a doe. What is all the fuss about anyway?

My legs were starting to get sore from four days of trying to push off the lower limbs with my boots barely touching. I spent much of the time now with my crotch pushed up against the tree uncomfortably. I stayed up in the tree until I heard our truck pull into camp and the doors open and close. It was so quite in the woods it sounded like it happened right next to me. I climbed out my tree and man was I happy to be on the ground again. It felt so good to get out of the tree and walk around. I vowed to go to bed early tonight so I wouldn't feel so tired again. Maybe tomorrow will be the day the buck comes back. Then again, maybe I am just trying to keep my hopes up for another day.

Day 5 - Wednesday, November 10, 1976

Everybody wanted to stay up late again last night and play cards. My Dad and Paul got even more tipsy than the night before. Dad even let my brother Johnny taste his beer. I'm pretty sure it wasn't his first time. Anyway, by 9:00 pm I was actually getting really tired and even a bit bored. I just wanted to go to bed but I didn't want to be teased and I certainly didn't want anybody mad at me. The card game our family plays more or less requires four people so if I had gone to bed, I would have spoiled their fun. I finally got to crawl into bed at around 11:00 pm. That meant when the alarm went off this morning I decided just to stay in my sleeping bag.

I could see everybody else was tired (and I'm pretty sure my Dad and my oldest brother were a bit hungover as well) but they got up anyway and started making breakfast. All I wanted to do was sleep for a little longer. I closed my eyes and when I opened them again everyone was gone and the sun was up. Man did I feel embarrassed. I just knew they were going to tease me to no end and call me a baby when they got back today.

The camper was freezing so I put my clothes on as best I could while staying in the sleeping bag. I'm pretty good at that on account of growing up where it can be super cold even inside. In the winter, I always keep my pants and a sweater beside the bed so I can put them on before I have to actually get out of bed. In any event, when I had my clothes on and sat up, I noticed a note on the table. I hurried over and read it and I immediately felt better. It read: "I know your tired son, get some rest this morning and then go get 'em tiger! Love Dad". It was only a handful of words but it made my day.

I felt inspired and so I decided to go out and stay in my oak tree for the rest of the day, even though it was just past 11:00 am. I packed a sandwich and some candy bars and stuffed two cans of Coke in my hunting jacket. I left a quick note for the others so they wouldn't worry about me. When I got to the tree, Old

Red was there to entertain me from time to time and Pretty Girl even showed up later in the afternoon to try to stop me thinking about time all the other stuff that was floating around in my head. As far as the hunting side goes, nothing really happened. To be honest, something else did.

I was thinking about the doe and the buck and all that nonsense about making fawns. At that time, my legs were so sore I just let them dangle and that pushed my crotch hard against the tree again. That's when it got really weird. All of the sudden, it actually felt kind of nice. 'Nice' isn't the right word and I don't know how I could ever describe it but I know I have never felt anything like it before. It felt wonderful. Then, I guess I started to feel guilty for it feeling like that. I've already had my first confession and all so I figured I could maybe include that one next time. Something about the sensation made me feel like it was definitely wrong even though, as I said before, it really felt wonderful. Still, from what I've learned, most things that feel good usually involve sinning in one way or another.

I didn't dare tell anybody about it when we got back to camp. Part of me was hoping it was just a one-off sort of thing and that it wouldn't *happen again. Then again, another part of me thought it was incredible. I've never had any talk about the birds and the bees but I can tell you there are kids in my Catholic school who can tell the craziest stories about girls. One guy, who I won't name, actually brought in a dirty magazine that he found under his father's bed. You wouldn't believe what was in it. At the time, I thought it was pretty disgusting. That night though, I kept thinking back about this one picture of this lady with these big boobs who was wearing lots of lipstick. When I thought about it, the same wonderful feeling started to come back until I closed my eyes and finally fell asleep. Who knows, maybe it all was just a dream. Talk about confusing. All I know is that I felt very ashamed of myself for even thinking about such things.*

* * *

Elton waited for almost an half hour before Robbie came out through the heavy glass doors at the back of the school. Earlier that day, Sister Gilbert had announced to the whole class that Robbie would be staying after school as his punishment. They usually walked home together, passing by the courthouse and then over an old, wooden railroad bridge. It took them across the river that carved its way through town, leaving behind rugged, clay cliffs in its wake. Once across, they would climb up a twisting pathway through the woods to the gravel road where they both lived a few houses apart from each other. When Robbie finally emerged, they walked in silence until they reached the railroad bridge.

"Did it hurt?" Elton asked, looking down through the gaps in the wooden railroad ties to the swirling water of the river far below.

"She didn't lay a finger on me," Robbie said.

"Sure, but what about her ruler?"

"Not that either."

"Than why'd she make you stay after?"

"She said she just wanted to talk to me."

"So she was only really trying to humiliate you in front of everyone by making you stay after."

"I'm not really sure. It was all a bit confusing to tell you the truth. She even gave me my book back on the condition that I didn't take it to school with me again."

"Which one was it?"

"*Slaughterhouse-Five.*"

"Is that one of those really naughty books?"

"You mean with kissing and that sort of thing?"

"And girls with loads of lipstick and big boobs

and all that. It was – wasn't it? Why else would Sister Gilbert get so cross at you."

"I swear it wasn't. There's some weird stuff like that in the book that I really don't get but that's not at all what it's about."

"What's it about then?"

"A lot of stuff you probably wouldn't like."

"Try me."

"Alright then. What if time wasn't actually sequential and you could choose which part of your life you wanted to be in whenever you wanted to be there?"

"You mean like I could fast forward to being all grown up and married."

"Something like that."

"That would be pretty cool. Could I go backwards in time as well as forward?"

"Any time you choose but everything would always be the same from when you were a baby to the day you died."

"What would be the same?"

"Absolutely everything you did, said, experienced – everything. Wouldn't you get bored?"

"I would just do something different," Elton said. Just then, he stumbled on one of the ties and then fell down hard onto the tracks. Robbie helped him back to his feet.

"You okay?" Robbie asked.

"I'm fine – Glad there's not a train due for another 15 minutes," Elton said. He brushed off his jeans and the front of his shirt.

"You're elbow's bleeding," Robbie said.

"It's nothing," Elton responded. He cupped his elbow with his other hand to stop the blood from getting on his shirt. "Really, I'm okay."

"That's perfect."

"What are you talking about?"

"Imagine if you could go back in time to the moment right before you just tripped."

"Then I'd make sure I was more careful and didn't trip next time. What are you on about?"

"That's the thing – what if you couldn't be more careful next time. What if all you did was experience the same event again, exactly the same way, no matter how many times you went back to that precise moment?"

"I don't think I'd like it at all."

"Supposedly, that's what it's like to be a *Tralfamadorian*."

"A what?"

"Those are the aliens in the book who experience time that way. In the end, they just choose the good bits of their lives."

"So why would Sister Gilbert get so mad at you for reading that? She must have read it herself."

"I don't think she has. I think she has just

heard bad things about it. It's full of lots of cursing, some naughty stuff, aliens and some really bad things about World War II. The main thing that scares people like her is the things I just told you about the *Tralfamadorians*."

"Why would that scare her?"

"I think the whole concept of nonlinear time scares a lot of people. Some people in the church even think it's anti-Christian but I don't see why."

"Nonlinear?"

"It's just means time might not be experienced in a straight line like we talked about before. We all seem to think everyone consciously experiences each moment in time everywhere in the universe together, one tick of the clock at a time."

"That's how it actually works," Elton said.

"What if that wasn't true? What if time and space were really linked together. Then we would end up with this bizarre four dimensional universe."

"Are you just trying to blow my mind or what?"

"No. I'm just telling you that was one of the things the book's about. You don't have to be Einstein to understand it," Robbie said. He stopped in the middle of the railroad bridge and took off his backpack, setting it across one of the railroad ties and pulling out the paperback.

"What are you doing?" Elton said. "We need to get across now. We're only half way and I don't' want to cut it close again like we did this spring. Don't forget, we're already late on account of that book."

"Hold your horses. I just want to read you something from it. This guy explains it way better than I can. Here it is," Robbie said, opening the book wider and holding it closer to his face.

"Hurry up," Elton said, a bit nervously.

"Alright, alright. This is what is says: *'I am a Tralfamadorian, seeing all time as you might see a stretch of the Rocky Mountains. All time is all time. It does not change. It does not lend itself to warnings or explanations. It simply is.'* Do you get it now?"

"To be perfectly honest – no. I really don't get it at all. And even if I did, I certainly don't see why anything you said would be anti-Christian even if it's super weird and you should really go see a child psychiatrist or something."

"It would only go against Christianity if you believe that thinking about the universe that way means you've taken away a person's freedom to choose right and wrong. I reckon that's just misunderstanding the whole concept of time."

"That's great," Elton said, now with more urgency. "Let's talk about it later. Put your backpack on and let's get the heck out of here. We're cutting it way too close."

"Take it easy, Elton. The next train shouldn't cross the bridge until 4:30 pm."

"Have you looked at your clock lately?"

"Holy crap!" Robbie said, pulling up his jacket sleeve and staring at his watch in disbelief. "I lost track of time," he said.

"It's all well and good with your Tralfamadorian time stuff but I don't think it is going to help us if we get run over by the Burlington Northern."

"You got that right. I'm pretty sure that the laws of physics don't' permit us to occupy the same space in time as a freight train no matter where in the universe we might be situated!"

After a few more steps, they heard two long, loud blasts of a horn. They both realized at once the train was heading towards them from the north. For Elton, he knew for certain because he knew what time it was and also the train schedule. For Robbie, he knew by listening to the sound of the blast of the train's horn. The very slight increase in pitch meant, according to the Doppler Effect, the sound waves were compressing relative to his position and thus causing them to increase in frequency.

"Double holy crap!" Elton yelled back to Robbie, who was only a few railroad ties behind him on the bridge. They still had more than a third of the bridge left to reach the other side. They froze for a moment as they saw the huge, dark-green locomotive engine round the corner a quarter mile from the bridge. Even with the train that far away, they could already begin to feel the railroad bridge start to vibrate from its incredible power.

"Are you thinking what I'm thinking," Robbie said.

"If you're thinking we're about to die – yes, we're on the same frickin' page!"

"We can't get across in time, we're going to have to jump into a gusset!"

"What's a gusset!"

"Just follow me for cripes' sake," Robbie screamed as the sound of the train grew louder and more ominous. He grabbed Elton by the hand and pulled him in the opposite direction towards the center of the railroad bridge.

"Are you nuts?"

"No, it's our only chance. We've got to climb down into the steel railing. Don't' freeze on me or this won't end well. There's no way for the engineer to stop even if he sees us!"

They heard the locomotive engineer blast his horn as he was about to come onto the bridge and then the brakes lock, grinding against the rails for a fraction of a second as he saw the two boys running towards the center of the bridge in front of him. With as many cars as he was pulling, the engineer knew at once there was no point in braking. He watched through the side window of the locomotive as the two boys raced away in front of the train.

Running on a railroad bridge is not possible for anyone without a great deal of experience. It requires you to run in evenly spaced strides so one of your feet doesn't come through between the railroad ties. If you misstep at pace, your leg goes down between the wooden ties and then snaps your shinbone. If you're lucky, one of the two bones in your lower leg survives. If not, you can break both lower legs bones at once. The pain of that happening and the risk of a compound fracture, where the bones go through the skin, is beyond description.

"Follow me!" Robbie screamed, jumping down off the main rail platform and down onto the steel girder railing to the side of the track. It was only about a yard below the tracks but there was nothing more between them and the river more than 50 feet below.

"I can't do it," Elton screamed as the train approached. By now the entire bridge was shaking with the sheer weight and force of the freight train.

"Grab my hand – I got you!"

Elton stuck his hand down below the rail and Robbie strong-armed him down onto the steel railing. In a moment, he helped Elton into a structural pocket in the railing that created a small space to crawl into and hide. Robbie had no time to climb in the one on the opposite side of the steel girder. He held onto the steel railing above him and felt the full force of the freight train as it passed. He lost his footings a few times as the railroad bridge shook with the fury of the train before they finally saw the last car pass and the vibrations begin to subside.

When the train had finally passed, Robbie was left standing on the steel railing below the main rail platform. His hands were gripped on the steel railing above his head and they were as white as he had ever seen them.

"What the heck am I sitting inside of?" Elton said.

"That, my friend, is a gusset. It forms a pocket where the different sections of steel railing are held together by heavy metal plates with rivets. And it's also the best place to hide when you get caught in the middle of the bridge."

"How'd you know about it?"

"My older brother Paul told me about it. He even made me sit in one while a train went over just to make sure I knew."

"I thought you told me Paul was really mean," Elton said.

"He is sometimes. Maybe even most of the times, but he's my brother. I think he feels he is the only one entitled to torment me. I think he still cares about me in a weird sort of brotherly way."

"I don't think I'll ever get this brotherhood thing," Elton said.

"Let's just be happy we're safe. Anyway, we need to get out of here quick in case the engineer calls the cops," Robbie said, helping Elton out of the gusset. They both climbed back up to the tracks from the steel railing below. Even that was dangerous given how hard it was to grab ahold of anything other than the railroad ties themselves.

"Would he really call the police?"

"One of them called the cops on Paul and I. It was my first and only chance to sit in the back of a police car. Paul said they were just trying to scare us but I'm never really scared when I'm with him, unless I'm actually alone with him and he's in one of his dark moods. Then it's best to just lock myself in the bathroom."

"Why don't you tell your Mom on him?"

"He's my brother so I don't really want him to get in trouble with her. He's got enough issues himself without me making it worse."

"Are you gonna tell your Mom about getting in trouble for reading the book?" Elton called ahead to Robbie, who was walking quickly now across the railroad ties in front of him.

"Yes – then she'll know why I'm late and all."

"Do you think she'll be upset that you were reading about the Tralfamadorians and stuff."

"Not at all. She's the one who gave me the book in the first place."

"So she's not even going to be upset at all with you?"

"She'll be upset alright, but just for me getting caught reading it during class. Don't forget, my Mom's the one who stopped the school board from banning '*The Hunchback of Notre Dame*' when she first came to town."

"How'd she do that?"

"She just took a pragmatic approach rather than trying to defend it."

"You and your frickin' words, Robbie. What do you mean by '*pragmatic*'?"

"It just means sort of practical under the circumstances."

"I've got news for you then, Robbie – that wasn't very *pragmatic* stopping and reading in the middle of the bridge like that."

"Sorry about that."

"No big deal. We're still alive and all. Anyway, what did your Mom end up doing that convinced them?"

"She asked them if they had read the book. She told them it was more than 900 pages long and the three volume set hadn't been checked out of the school library in more than 15 years."

"Why would she really care anyway?"

"My Mom's just different. I think her favorite book is this one called *'Fahrenheit 451'*. She made me read it last year. That's supposedly the temperature when paper catches fire if you want to burn books and all that. She said you didn't need to burn books if you just found a way to stop people from reading them. I think she just loved books and thought they were really important."

"Even so, I still can't believe Sister Gilbert would give you your book back even if you told her all that," Elton said, as they finally reached the end of the railroad bridge.

"I never told her all that," Robbie said.

"So why in the world do you think she gave it back then?"

"I'm still not really sure. Sister Gilbert told me I should really be ashamed of myself for reading in class. I knew that part was coming and I was doing my best to feel suitably ashamed. But then she said she also wanted to tell me that I was '*gifted*' and that she expected great things from me."

"What'd you say?"

"I told her I was just reading a stupid book."

* * *

Day 6 - Thursday, November 11, 1976

Today, I almost managed to kill myself. I didn't try to do it but it was still darn close. The day started out normal enough - at least by deer camp standards. I forced myself to get out of bed even before the alarm went off and then started making breakfast right away for everyone. Just the basics, scramble eggs and bacon and some cut up oranges. I wanted to try to make up for how bad I felt inside for not getting up with everyone yesterday. Maybe I was even trying to make up for the weird things I had been thinking about. To tell you the truth, that strange sensation I had and all the thoughts that went with it seemed pretty gross to me when I woke up and I felt again ashamed for having them.

Anyway, I resolved that I wasn't going to think like that anymore and I was going to make sure that I pushed off on the branches with my feet so I wouldn't end up scrunched up *against the tree trunk ever again. I didn't manage to get out to the oak tree until just after sunrise on account of I also decided to do the dishes after the others left camp. I even tidied up the camper so it would be clean when everyone came back for lunch. I don't know about you but I always feel good about myself when I'm cleaning up things.*

I was searching desperately for a way to feel good about myself and get rid of this guilty feeling. It made me feel sick to my stomach in real life. I just hoped the buck hadn't decided to take advantage of me being late and walk across the meadow before I could climb the oak tree.

The morning was bright orange with the sun coming up just above the tree tops behind me and I could see across the meadow. I couldn't see any knew footprints and the woods were very quiet like they'd been the last couple of days. Still, I didn't even see or hear Old Red or Pretty Girl the whole morning.

At about mid-morning, I heard three rifle shots about a half mile or so off to the west. My first thought was that someone had shot my buck if he hadn't been shot already. But even if he was already shot, who's to say that another buck might not just come across the meadow anyway. I could see a perimeter of almost a 150 yards in each direction. The only problem was my sawed off 20 gauge with heavy slugs. Like Dad told me, it wouldn't be much use unless it was within about 50 yards.

By 11:00 am, my legs were shaking from pushing off on the lower branches. I shifted from one side to the other to try to give one leg a rest at a time and also so my butt didn't hurt so bad on the main branch. Eventually I had to give my legs a rest and you can guess what that meant. Once again, I was pushed up uncomfortably into the tree trunk. I was getting used to it by now and sure enough my mind began to wander. I was so tired and weird images started popping up in my head. I might have even thought about my teacher for a moment. How sick is that? Pretty soon the weird sensation started again but I was so tired from being up late that I started to fall asleep. I startled myself awake a couple of times but soon I was clearly in dreamland. I don't even remember exactly what I was dreaming about but maybe I'm not being totally honest.

Anyway, that's when I almost managed to kill myself or at least hurt myself very badly. My rifle was hanging above me from a branch *just above eye level on the side of the tree. After what happened on the first day, I made sure the branch was strong enough so that I would never drop my shotgun again. The problem was that it was the only branch I could hold onto. Otherwise, I had to wrap my arms around the tree. I don't know how long I was asleep but I will never forget the moment I woke up. I was falling over sideways and was at a 45 degree angle and about to do a face plant into the branches below me. Instinctively, I grabbed for the branch my gun was hanging on to stop myself from falling over.*

That's when everything got a bit more scary. The branch broke off and the gun came with it. I managed to catch the nylon rope tied to the butt of the shotgun but only just after it smashed into my forehead. I was lucky I didn't get knocked out when it hit me or, even worse, that it would have gone off. If either of those things happened, I'm not sure I would be able to write this now. I ended up with my legs wrapped around the main branch hanging upside down, with my forehead bleeding and the shotgun dangling from the nylon rope in my hand. I'll never forget hanging there looking at the woods upside down. It gave me a very practical perspective about the thoughts I was having about time and space!

I don't know how I managed to get myself back seated on the branch but I know it took a lot of effort. There was just enough of a stub of the branch left at eye level to hang the shotgun. My heart was still racing like a madman. As soon as I caught my breath, I climbed down from the tree and headed straight back to camp. The bleeding wasn't too bad but I had a big, purple lump on my forehead. I knew when my brothers saw me they were really gonna tease me once they knew I was okay and all. I just had to take it. I can't help but think that God was punishing me for having those bad thoughts. I made a note to myself to make certain I went to confession as soon as I got back home. I really wanted my soul to feel all fresh and clean again.

Day 7 - Friday, November 12, 1976

Today didn't turn out anything like I had planned but man was it exciting. I made it out to the oak tree before 7:00 am and the conditions were great. There was just enough wind so that it wasn't too quite but not so much that you couldn't hear anything. A light *snow was falling which always makes it easier to see fresh tracks. I had already seen Old Red and heard Pretty Girl behind me and was just starting to feel sore from being in the same position for a couple hours. Then I heard a car pull into camp and my Dad's voice call out "Robbie!" I was out of my tree in no time and almost jogged back to camp once I got to the trail.*

'What's up?' I said when I saw my Dad waiting by the car.

'Johnny shot one but it didn't go down. We're tracking it over in the big woods south of the road. I want you to be with Son'.

''I wouldn't miss it for the world!' I said.

'Get in, then,' he said.

We drove off and met up with my older brother at the road. He told us Johnny was in the woods waiting at the last blood sign. We all made our way across the ditch which was easy on account of it being frozen and then followed my older brother's boot prints until we met up with Johnny about a half mile into the woods. When we met him he was in a bit of distress and Dad tried to calm him down.

'How could I possibly screw up that shot - he was literally broadside 70 yards away from me.'

'Don't torture yourself,' Dad said. 'From what I can tell from how he's bleeding, he's lung shot and they can go a few miles but not more. You don't have to miss the heart by much to be in this situation.'

'Still Dad - I have been at the range every day for the last two weeks and I can always hit the bullseye.'

'Buck fever,' Paul teased. 'It can turn even the best shooter into a jiggling bowl of jello.'

'Listen Boys,' Dad said. 'Concentrate on the task at hand. We have a good blood trail and we're just going to keep on it until we get this buck and bring it back to camp. That's a hunter's duty whenever you wound an animal. Nobody tries to do it but it does happen. Now let's get a move on it.'

I don't think Sister Gilbert has probably ever tracked a wounded deer before but it works really well when you're more than one person. I was assigned to be the one who waited at the last blood sign while my older brothers and my Dad searched for the next one. When they found it and it was confirmed, then I would walk up to the next blood sign and wait there until they found another. That process just goes on and on until you get closer to the deer. If it stops bleeding then you are in big trouble, especially if it gets in with other deer or on a trail that's used a lot. If it keeps bleeding, eventually you will catch up to it and either find it already down or you'll get close enough to shoot it and put it out of its misery.

The problem we had was that a lung-shot deer doesn't bleed very much. We did have fresh snow so it was easier than it could have been. In the end, the blood sign they were finding wasn't even in the snow, it was on brush that had rubbed against its side. After a mile or so, we knew exactly what height the bullet wound was at and Dad said he was certain it was in fact shot in the lungs. The thing is it takes a long time to make any progress and by 3:30 pm we were starting to lose light and we really needed to catch up to the deer quickly. Dad walked straight ahead and put my older brothers 100 yards to either side of him so the deer wouldn't keep on doubling back on us.

Sure enough, while I was waiting at the last blood sign about 100 yards behind them, I heard a loud rifle shot go off to the left where Johnny should have been. Then I heard Dad yell 'Get him?' and my brother immediately respond 'He's down!' I wasn't supposed to leave the last blood sign until Dad told me I could *but I just ran ahead anyway. I don't think I have ever seen Johnny so happy in all my life. I was happy for him too - it was a big 8 point buck.*

By the time we had dragged the deer out to the road, it was dark on account of my Dad let Johnny field dress his deer. I felt really good for him but I have to confess I was a little jealous even though, as I said before, when you get a deer in camp it feels like everyone got it. This time that was really true because we all had to work together to track it. We had fulfilled our duty as hunters and that made me feel good too. I was also happy not to have to sit up in the oak tree all day, being uncomfortable and thinking weirdo thoughts. The only problem was that now we had three deer in camp and only one deer tag left that any of us could fill. Fingers crossed it's me next time even if any one of us are still allowed to shoot it.

* * *

School started an hour later than usual due to the heavy snowfall overnight. The snow had arrived much later than the people of northern Minnesota were accustomed to and, to be brutally honest, most were starting to feel guilty for having life a bit too easy. The arrival of the heavy snow up north had a welcome and almost cathartic effect on people, presumably not unlike the coming of the summer monsoons in India. Nature had shown once again it was well aware of the seasons. For most residents of the town, the world was once again coming into order.

Robbie arrived early to school, having walked across the railroad bridge rather than wait for the bus to show up. As he crossed the bridge, his boots crunched into the eight inches of snow resting on top of the railroad ties. He knew this meant school would be cancelled or, at a minimum, be delayed for a few hours as the buses tried to round up the country kids. The riverbanks below the bridge were coated in a blanket of white with the clay cliffs to the north rising above them untouched. Despite the freezing temperatures, the dark water of the river still flowed through the channel as he watched the swirling snowflakes descend and then melt instantly upon touching the surface.

Sister Gilbert was alone at her desk drinking a mug of tea when he arrived. She had managed to trek across the snow-covered playground earlier that morning from the convent on the other side of the school. When Robbie unexpectedly opened the door, she seemed to be enjoying the quietness of the classroom in what would otherwise have been a hectic Monday.

"Is school still on today, Sister?"

"Oh Robbie – you're back," Sister Gilbert replied warmly. "The plows were out early but the wind is still blowing the snow across the roads. I don't know if the country children are going to make it in at all."

"I guess I'll just wait," Robbie said, unzipping his parka. He went to the cloakroom and hung all his outer clothing on the hook provided. As he was pulling off his snow boots, he stared at the placard above his hook with "Robbie" written in orange, handwritten letters. Quite suddenly, the sign made him feel very babyish. He waited a moment before emerging from the cloakroom, hoping some of the other students might arrive before he had to face Sister Gilbert again.

"Come here," Sister Gilbert said before Robbie could seat himself at his desk. "Don't worry, I don't bite."

"What is it, Sister?" Robbie said, hurriedly closing the top of his desk. He was quite certain she had not seen him place the envelope inside.

"You've been gone for more than a week and I want you to hear all about your hunting trip or would you rather that I wait and read your journal instead?"

"The diary?" Robbie said. He could feel his face going bright red, even more so than when he had walked in out of the cold.

"Your assignment. I've been looking forward to reading it. You have written it, haven't you?"

Robbie looked down at his feet as he walked tentatively towards her desk. He struggled with what to say even though he had rehearsed it in his head more times than he could remember over the weekend. "Yes. The diary," he stammered. "I didn't quite finish it just yet. You could say it's kind of a work in progress, Sister."

"You did keep one as we agreed, though didn't you?"

"Oh yes, Sister. I kept one alright." He had hesitated slightly before responding and then shifted his weight back and forth on his feet slowly, as if balancing on a teeter-totter.

"In writing?"

"Yes, in manner of speaking."

"I'm quite certain a student with your overgrown vocabulary knows the difference between writing and speaking. Have you or have you not *written* a diary, young man? I want a straight answer this time," Sister Gilbert said.

"It's all written. It's just that it's all inside my head at the moment, Sister."

"Don't you get smart with me. So what you're telling me is that you actually haven't written down a single word yet?"

Robbie stared down at the floor. He could feel his face turning red and feel tears starting to well up in eyes. He wished a trap door underneath him would suddenly open and he would simply disappear forever. Better still, he tried to imagine himself casually looking away from this dreadful moment each time he needed to cross over it to find a happier one to dwell upon.

"Answer me!"

"No, Sister," Robbie said. "I haven't written down anything."

"You should be ashamed of yourself, young man," Sister Gilbert said, her voice shaking with anger.

"I promise I'll have it all done by the end of this week, Sister."

"Your promises mean very little because you don't keep them. You promised me you would keep a diary and that you would turn it in as soon as you were back from the trip. That was the one condition I told you to tell your father was necessary in order for me to give you permission to miss so much school. What do you think he is going to say when I tell him you didn't even bother to do the one assignment I gave you?"

"I honestly don't think he'll actually care, Sister."

"I know you're father and I am pretty sure he will be quite upset with you."

"I don't think you know my father as well as you think, Sister. I don't think he would be mad at me at all, especially since I never told him I was supposed to write a diary in the first place."

"Shame on you, Robbie. How could not tell your father like I told you to do?"

"Sister, if I would've told him, I'm pretty sure it would have created more trouble for us."

"How could that possibly be?"

"He doesn't think he needs to tell you anything if he wants to take me hunting. He said he thinks it's even more important for me to spend a week out in the woods with my family then going to school."

"What in the world does he think you're going to learn in the woods that's going to be more important than what you would have learned in school for an entire week."

"I don't know, Sister. Just stuff. I don't want to cause a fight between you two."

"Then you should of simply written the diary. I'm calling your father."

"Please don't, Sister."

"And I was even looking forward to reading it. You always write such interesting things."

"I'm sorry, Sister. I'm just so sorry."

"Well, it's a little late for that now. I want you to go back to your desk and start writing a letter to God asking him for forgiveness. You can finish it and give it to me before you go home whether or not school is cancelled."

The door to the class room opened just as Robbie was turning to walk back to his desk. Elton stood in the doorway with his glasses fogged over from the cold and then quickly disappeared into the cloak room without saying a word. When he emerged, Elton sat down at his desk located right beside Robbie's.

"She didn't buy it?" he whispered.

"I don't want to talk about it," Robbie said, staring blankly at a single sheet of paper he had taken out from under his desk.

"That bad, huh?"

"I said, I don't want to talk about it."

"I take it that was one of those moments that a Tralfamadorian wouldn't be focusing on too often."

"You got that right," Robbie said.

Robbie stared down at the blank sheet of paper for a long time with a sharpened pencil in his hand. No matter how hard he tried, he could never get any farther than "Dear God."

* * *

Day 8 - Saturday, November 14, 1976

Today was, without a doubt, the weirdest day of my life so far. For starters, I looked in the mirror this morning in the bathroom we're not supposed to use and saw that I actually had a few whiskers on my chin and on the sides of my mouth. I definitely need to shave for the first time when we get back home. I didn't really think too much about it but I found out later from Johnny that all this stuff that's going on is somehow connected. That wasn't even the crazy bit of the day.

I know I'm gonna have to cross all this stuff out but I am going to tell you what actually happened. I went to the oak tree after lunch, hoping the buck would finally show up. I hadn't heard or seen anything the whole morning other than Old Red and a rabbit that was half white sitting by a brush pile almost right below my tree. It's the last weekend so I didn't even bother giving it a name. The last weekend is always the hardest because the deer are unsettled from all the hunters and shooting. Still, we had one tag left and I still believed that buck was finally going to come back to his rut to find his girlfriend and I was going to be waiting for him.

The sun was shining and it was a warm afternoon. I sat in the tree daydreaming after eating a big lunch. I was tired but there was no way I was going to end up hanging upside down from that branch again. My eyes maybe closed a few times but I had a huge adrenaline kick because of what happened and that made me wide awake again. My legs were so sore from pushing off the lower branches all week I just let them dangle. To tell you the truth, I didn't mind so much being pushed up against the tree again. As soon as I did though, all those weirdo thoughts started coming back again.

The funny thing was, the sensation kept on feeling better and better and my weirdo thoughts kept on going and even getting more dirty. I felt guilty but I didn't really care anymore because it started to feel so incredible. After a while, I stopped even caring about whether that stupid deer was going to finally come out into the meadow. Instead, I just felt this wonderful feeling growing inside me. It was almost like my whole body was tingling. I guess I don't even know what words to use to actually describe how it felt.

Then it happened. Just when I thought it couldn't possibly feel any nicer and my thoughts couldn't get any dirtier, something absolutely crazy happened. All of a sudden, my parts that were pushed against the tree started pulsating like crazy. After a moment, the wonderful sensation went away, together with all the dirty thoughts. I panicked because I was pretty sure I had just damaged something badly. All because of the stupid way I was sitting and all those stupid, weirdo, wicked thoughts.

I was so scared, I almost fell out of the tree trying to get down on the ground as soon as possible. I jumped down the last eight feet or so, shotgun in hand. I had to even roll to break the fall. When I stood up my chest was pounding so hard I thought I might be having a heart attack or something. I was even more certain I had broken something down there. My underpants felt wet so I quickly unbuckled my belt, pulled down my hunting pants and unbuttoned my long underwear. I was expecting to see blood but it wasn't blood or anything like that.

I couldn't imagine how I was ever going to explain to anyone how I managed to hurt myself so badly. I stood there thinking of a way to describe it without talking about the weirdo thoughts and all. I could say it just happened when I was sitting there for no reason at all. That I had no control over it. But I was such a bad liar. My brothers would spot it in less than a second and so would Elton.

That's when things got even more crazy. I was standing there catching my breath with my pants still pulled down and rehearsing in my mind how I was going to tell people that I accidentally hurt myself. Suddenly, I heard the brush snap towards the end of the meadow. There was no way it was Old Red or Pretty Girl or even the rabbit. Sure enough, at that very moment the big buck I had been waiting for all week walked out into the meadow and stopped. He had huge horns and was standing broadside not more than 30 yards from me. I clicked off the safety on the sawed off 20 gauge and pointed it towards the deer. My hands were shaking like a madman and my heart was pounding so hard I thought my chest would explode at any moment. Now I really knew what 'buck fever' meant.

I took a deep breath and lined up the barrel directly at the spot we were taught to shoot at. The spot was just behind the foreleg where the slug would enter the chest cavity and hopefully hit the heart. I squeezed the trigger in anticipation of the sound of the shotgun firing. Instead, what I heard was simply a click. I was shocked and confused and didn't manage to load another shell into the chamber before the buck walked off across the end of the meadow and into the woods. By then it was too late to shoot again because I was on the ground and the brush blocked me from seeing him. Had I been in my tree, I would have still been able to see him.

I unloaded the shotgun shell from the chamber. The firing pin had hit the primer and left a dent in it but hadn't caused the shell to fire. I leaned my shotgun against the tree and then buttoned my long underwear and pulled up my hunting pants. I could only come to one conclusion. God was punishing me for all my bad and evil thoughts and what happened in that tree. Why else would the buck come out just then after me waiting there for an entire week? And why else would the shotgun shell not fire when I had a perfect shot at him? I'd never seen a shell that didn't fire before and the only conclusion I could come up with was that God was incredibly and unforgivably angry with me.

I walked back to camp then feeling very sad and totally ashamed of myself. I knew that if I was a Tralfamadorian this would be a moment in time I would hop over every chance I got. I was still scared to death that I had damaged myself and I've never felt so much guilt in all my life. A thousand sincere and heartfelt confessions would never be enough to fix a sin this horrible!

At the same time, I admit I was also sort of mad at God for not letting me get the deer. Why in the world did the stupid buck have to show up right then after I had spent so many hours waiting for him? As much as I hate to write this on paper, I began to think that God was being a bit of a bully. I have to be honest like I said I was going to be with this diary and confess that what happened did feel wonderful until I damaged myself. Why does everything that feels so good have to be some sort of big sin all the time? 'So it goes.'

Day 9 - Sunday, November 15, 1976

All's well that ends well, especially when you already know how it all ends. That was sure true for me today. After yesterday, just about anything that happened would be better but now I feel like I just won the lottery! At first no one believed me last night when I told them about what happened in the meadow - I mean with the deer and all. Not the other stuff. But then I showed them the shell with the dent in the primer and I knew they believed me. Dad asked why I was standing on the ground and I just said it was because I was really sore from sitting up in the oak tree for so many days. Of course, I didn't mention my pants were down. It was a bit of a lie but I couldn't exactly tell him what really happened. Would you?

The only person I thought I might be able to tell was Johnny. I had to tell someone that I was damaged in case I died or something in the middle of the night. We were both putting our hunting gear in the tent before going in the camper where my Dad and oldest brother were making dinner.

I finally just blurted out, 'Something really weird happened to me Johnny.'

'What's that?'

'I was sitting in the tree and then I think I damaged myself.'

'What are you talking about? What do you mean you damaged yourself?'

'I accidentally hurt myself.'

'Where?'

'My private parts,' I whispered. 'I damaged my private parts, Johnny.'

'What do you mean by damaged?'

'I was just sitting there and then some things happened and then...'

'And then what?'

And then my private parts started going all crazy. I was thinking dirty thoughts and all and I was kind of pushed up against the stupid tree trunk.'

'You dork. You just had a wet dream for the first time.'

'What do you mean? I wasn't even asleep.'

'Get used to it - you're growing up now. It's what happens. It's called 'ejaculation'. That just shows you're turning into a grown man. You haven't damaged yourself at all so stop worrying about that already.'

'Are you sure?'

'Yes, I'm sure - hasn't anybody told you that was gonna happen?'

'No. Not really.'

'You'll be fine you little rodent. It's just natural. With as much as you read, you'd think you would have come across it by now.'

'I have read about stuff like that by I never knew how it happened.'

'Well, that's how it happens. Get over it already.'

I could have hugged him right then and there but I didn't. I can't begin to tell you how relieved I felt. It was like someone had taken the weight of the Earth off my shoulders. I thought I was the only one in the world who had ever done something so wicked. I'm not even going to tell you who I was thinking about because it's way too embarrassing. I still felt guilty but I was no longer certain I was going straight to hell for what happened when I was having all those weirdo thoughts.

Anyway, Dad said last night we could hunt this morning but that we had to pack up camp this afternoon because he needed to work the next day and we needed to get back to school. In other words, this morning was our last chance and we had one deer tag left. I was up in the oak tree well before first light. It felt strange climbing up it again after the way I came down it yesterday. One thing was for sure, under no circumstances was I going to sit improperly or have any weirdo thoughts. This morning I was fully concentrating on deer hunting and nothing else.

As if to say goodbye, Old Red and Pretty Girl both made appearances before 8:00 am. I tried

SPF Cameron

to ignore them and concentrate on the meadow. After yesterday, I even had my shotgun in my hands rather than hanging from the branch. The woods were beautiful in the first light of day. The sun was out again and everything seemed to almost glow in natural beauty. I felt thankful for the whole trip even if it hadn't gone to plan. It was just nice to connect to nature and feel a part of everything.

Then it happened. I heard a loud crunch coming from behind me. It was coming from the same direction as the doe had earlier and not towards end of the meadow where I had been looking. Once again, it was directly behind me and I had a hard time turning around my head to see anything let alone to be able to take a shot. I heard a few more crunches in the brush and knew it was a deer and that it was heading towards me from behind. I craned my neck around just enough to catch a glimpse of it. The first thing I saw was its antlers and I'm pretty sure it was the same deer as yesterday.

My hands started shaking and my heart started pounding in my chest again. The only chance I had was to stay super still and hope he took the same path as the doe had through the meadow. I was pretty sure he would hear the sound of my heart beating. I tried to take a few deep breaths to calm down. The crunches became louder as he approached until it sounded like he was almost directly under the tree behind me. A few more steps and I could literally look down at his back.

I switched off my safety as he entered the meadow. He must have heard the click because he stopped dead in his tracks. He was facing away from me and I was above him so I could shoot down at him. It wasn't ideal but I knew if I shot him in the middle of the base of the neck he would go down. I aimed the barrel of the sawed off shotgun down at him with my hands still shaking and squeezed the trigger. This time it was followed by a huge boom and then the buck dropped down immediately. He didn't even move. It was as if he just went to sleep.

I was supposed to wait for 15 minutes before coming down from the tree to make sure he died and that I didn't rouse him and give him a kick of adrenaline so that he would get up and run off. I could tell though he was dead. I could see the entry wound right in the middle of the base of his neck. After about 5 minutes, I climbed down from the tree. When

I walked over to him I was so excited but then I began to feel really guilty because I had just killed a huge, beautiful animal but then I quickly counted the points on its antlers. It was an 11 point buck and that was the biggest one this year.

Dad and my brothers eventually showed up after they heard the shot to help me field dress the buck and drag it out. I was so proud and I could see they were actually really happy for me. I confessed to Dad and my brothers that I felt a bit guilty about shooting it. It was just out in the woods doing what deer do and I ended its life. Dad said if you just kill something out in nature for no reason at all, then you're right you should feel guilty. Then he said to remember that this deer was going to feed our family all winter and that as long as you do that, you should never feel guilty about it. After he said that, I felt a lot better about everything.

My first deer hunting trip was over and I was no longer a greenhorn. I didn't exactly hunt so much as spend a lot of time sitting in an oak tree thinking about stuff in a way I never had before. I suppose you're never gonna read this Sister Gilbert, but I thought about some things you would be ashamed of me for, *including time, space, nature, boys and girls, even sex (as embarrassing as it is to write that).*

Still, I did get a deer and learned all sorts of things I hadn't planned on learning on this trip. I think the last day was one of the happiest of my life so far. I am looking forward to getting back to school so I can tell the other guys in my class what happened, especially Elton. Not about the weirdo thoughts, of course, but about shooting my first deer and all the other exciting things that happened.

THE END"

* * *

Harini watched from the kitchen as Jonathan closed the diary, placed it in his lap and removed his glasses. He wiped his eyes a few times and she could see, not for the first time, that he had been crying. She walked over and stood beside his chair. By now the fire was reduced to a hot-red glowing bed of embers.

"Are you okay?" she asked after a moment.

Jonathan wiped his eyes and took a few deep breaths. "I'm fine sweetheart," he said.

"Was it that sad?"

"Not really. Lots of happy memories and so many things I had forgotten."

81

"Why does that make you feel sad?"

"We should've talked more in our family. Not just idle words but about important things. The poor little guy carried so much guilt and shame all the time. I don't think it ever left him and I certainly never thought about it enough to say anything."

"Yes, but the hunting trip must have been a happy time together, wasn't it?"

"No doubt. It was a happy time. If Robbie had his way, that's all there would ever be. I just think we shouldn't have left him to himself so much. I should've taken him with me to the big woods that year rather than just leaving him hunting alone around camp."

"He was a bit of a loner so I'm sure he wouldn't have minded too much."

"Robbie wasn't always like that."

"Then why did he change? The times I met him, Robbie was always trying to be so positive even if he was shy to a fault."

"I know and that's really what's upsetting."

"Why would that be so upsetting to make you cry?"

Jonathan paused a moment to pull himself together. He looked about the room and tried to imagine his brother there. He could so easily picture him seated at his desk, writing with a warming fire burning beside him. "Because, like

I said, I remember that whole hunting trip now. The diary brought everything back to me with the clarity of a Proustian moment."

"What did you remember?"

"We only got three deer that year, not four like Robbie wrote in his diary. The biggest was a ten point buck my older brother Paul shot. I remember because he had it mounted and he never stopped bragging about getting the biggest deer. Paul always kidded that I should call him '*Bwana*' in Swahili or '*Great White Hunter*' after that season."

"Well, that was a pretty good year then. Three deer for a hunting party of four sounds good to me anyway."

"It's just that we did go out before packing up camp on the last day, but nobody shot anything."

"I'm still not following you?"

"Robbie always wanted his stories to be happy no matter what may have really happened."

"Okay, I still don't get it but, regardless, why didn't he at least turn the diary in to his teacher so he wouldn't get in trouble?"

"I think you probably need to read the diary to understand. I'm not sure what Robbie would have wanted but I trust you."

Jonathan picked up the diary from his lap and handed it to Harini. As he did so, a folded piece of notepaper slipped out from between the blank pages towards the end and landed in his lap. Harini took the diary from him while he opened up the note in a hurried fashion. After looking at it for a moment, he looked up at Harini in disbelief.

"What is it?"

"It's addressed to me from Robbie but I can't find any date. I can tell it's pretty recent though."

"How recent?"

"I'm not really sure. He did it on his computer but he signed it. I can see his signature is very shaky – it's even worse than his Christmas card last year."

"Yes, I remember that. We were both so worried because we had trouble even reading it. Nothing like the cards he used to send. What does it say?"

"Like I said, it's addressed to me. Maybe I should just give it a quick read first."

"Go ahead then. I can wait."

He opened the note and read it, mumbling from time to time as he had been doing when he read the diary before.

* * *

'Dear Johnny,

I know you will find this one day and I presume when you read it I will no longer be with you. I would have said this to you in person but you know how impossible that would have been for me.

I accept my capacity to think and write will soon be gone. Without them, I having nothing left to accompany me into old age. I assure you this is not meant to diminish in any way how much I care about you and your family and how much you have all meant to me. With Paul long since gone, I'm afraid you will be all that's left now of our family.

Despite my palsied hands, modern technology could surely find a way for me to write. I would have preferred to write this letter to you by hand but even that is no longer possible. My condition is taking away not only my capacity to write now but also my mind. As it departs, as I know it inevitably will, all the memories and imagination that have made life worth living will surely depart with it.

I hope you will forgive me but now I prefer to make that moment in time more precise. That way I can avoid it. I know from then on I will be able to spend eternity reliving those happy moments I have experienced during my life. Many of those, though long ago, were spent with you. How fun it is going to be to see those moments again and skip over all the not so happy ones.

This disease is about losing things and my mind is the last intimate companion I have left. The time and effort it takes to write a sentence feels the same as writing a chapter would have just a few years ago. I confess it has been difficult to endure the physical hardship of this disease. I can begrudgingly handle all that sort of thing but not the loss of my intellect.

Imagine looking out at an opulent landscape in spring, with colorful flowers and a radiant sun shining over the hills. And then, little-by-little, the sky darkens, the flowers lose their vibrant colors, the sun disappears behind the hills and the once beautiful landscape is transformed into featureless shapes in an ashen shade of gray before nightfall. Such is the state of my mind now as this insidious monster inside me takes control.

I want to thank you for being my brother and also let you know why I ended up living my life in solitude. I assure you it is not your fault or anyone's for that matter. I believe it happens to many people that are scarred by guilt and shame. Some people are able to overcome it. Others can't. I was unfortunately one of those who couldn't live around others because of the shame I felt all the time about myself. I left the diary for you alone to read so that you might understand one day where it all seemed to begin for me.

Long ago, I decided to marry myself to my writing rather than to a real person to avoid hurting anyone. But now my beloved spouse, wracked by the heinous and progressive dementia this illness brings, is leaving me. Like an old couple that cannot bear the thought of being apart, I choose to go with her. Don't be sad for me though. Just remember my favorite quote from my favorite book will also be foremost in my mind: '*Everything was beautiful and nothing hurt.*'

Please know that you were the one light, together with your family, that lit the world up outside my door. I shall never forget you. My only wish is that when you think of all the times we have had together, you choose to think like a true Tralfamadorian and only choose those times that were the happiest. Just those moments, over and over again. I know that's what I plan to do.

Your loving brother,

Robbie

P.S. When you are finished reading the diary, can you please give it the *Ray Bradbury* treatment for me, together with this note. I only kept the diary all these years for you to read and I can't let anyone know that what happened to me was not an accident."

* * *

Once he had finished reading, Jonathan set the note down on his lap and once again rubbed his eyes absent-mindedly. He stared at the happy photos on the mantel above the fireplace for a while without saying anything.

"Are you okay?" Harini asked.

"I'm fine."

"What did he say?"

"He was just saying goodbye in his own way."

"He must have written something more important than that. I just don't get it."

"Alright, there was one thing I think I should share."

"What?"

"You know how everyone always said Robbie was so painfully shy? Why didn't anybody, including me, ever stop and try to understand why he was like that?"

"Lots of people are shy. It doesn't mean there's something wrong with them," Harini said.

"I'm not saying there's something wrong with being shy in itself. Like you said, lots of people are. It's just that extreme shyness could be a sign of something deeper."

"Like what?"

"Feeling guilt all the time, perhaps. But I read that guilt can actually be a healthy thing. It supposedly means you haven't lived up to standards you've set for yourself. Shame's an entirely different matter."

"Why would shame be so different? I've always thought of guilt and shame as being basically the same thing?"

"I think in Robbie's case shame became so deeply imbedded in his self-image it went far beyond feeling guilty. It's one thing to feel guilty, which is basically feeling you're doing something wrong. Shame is so much worse because it's not about feeling you've done something wrong, but rather that there's something wrong with *you* as a human being. That's where his escapism probably really started."

"What could Robbie have done that was so bad that he felt ashamed for his entire life?"

"Nothing. That's the sad thing – he didn't do anything that every boy in history hasn't experienced in one way or another growing up. It's not what he did. It's that he wasn't prepared for it because no one told him it was going to happen and that it was okay."

"Oh," Harini said, "now I know what you're talking about. That helps explain something about Robbie that was really bothering me."

"What's that?"

"Do you remember when we sent the boys up to visit Robbie a few years back when he seemed to be going through some very dark depression."

"Of course I do. We thought it would cheer him up and hopefully give the boys a chance to get to know their Uncle Robbie. Never mind it would give them a chance to do some real fishing on Lake of the Woods rather than in the overstocked ponds down by the Cities."

"Precisely."

"You never told me anything bad happened then."

"I don't think anything really did. It was just a bit weird for the boys."

"How so?"

"Arjun told me that when Robbie was driving them down to Grand Forks to catch the Amtrak train to Minneapolis, he started an awkward conversation with them about the birds and the bees."

"I remember picking them up at the old Union Depot in St. Paul. I don't remember them saying anything about it though."

"Arjun probably only felt comfortable talking about it with me for whatever reason."

"How did the boys react?"

"Arjun just tried to change the subject right away but Robbie supposedly insisted on making sure he got his message across to them. Arjun said it was just so embarrassing. Apparently, that didn't seem to bother Robbie. When he finally stopped talking, Arjun said it was total silence in the car until they got to the Amtrak station."

"Good for Robbie for at least trying."

"Come on Jonathan," Harini said. "What kid today with a mobile phone doesn't know everything there is to know about sex and then some. By time time our boys were 12, they had probably already seen more of that sort of thing then we did by the time we were 30."

"I probably should have told you this before but I accidentally found some things on Arjun's phone around that time."

"Accidentally?"

"Well, sort of accidentally."

"What's that supposed to mean?"

"I was just worried about what he might be seeing after everything I've heard about kids and the internet these days. I wasn't trying to be a snoop or anything."

"How dare you, Jonathan."

"Let's just say I can confirm what you said about mobile phones and all that. I'll bet it's just about as confusing as what Robbie went through, only in a different way in the extreme."

"I still don't know precisely what Robbie went through," Harini said.

"It's all in the diary and I think that's where Robbie wanted it to stay."

"What about the note?"

"Like I said, it's just Robbie saying goodbye and some final instructions. Could you give me the diary back," he said, getting up from the chair.

"I'd like to read it if I can one day," she said, handing the diary to him and placing her hand gently on his shoulder.

"We can always talk about it as much as we want. Who knows, maybe we can even ask him about it one day. I suppose it depends on time and space and whoever you think might have got that one right."

Harini thought for a moment and then smiled at Jonathan. "I believe my Aachi was a very wise person."

"From what you've told me, she truly must have been. Then again, so was Einstein – not to mention people like Jules Verne, Richard Bach, Stephen Hawking, Robert Pirsig and, Robbie's favorite, Kurt Vonnegut. And that's still before we've even begun to scratch the universe of human thought on time and space."

"Who could possibly be certain," Harini said. She let her hand fall off of Jonathan's shoulder.

"Maybe that is where the concept of faith began in the first place," Jonathan said.

Harini watched as he unfolded the note from Robbie and placed it carefully between the pages of the diary. He then held the diary in both hands for a moment before opening it to the first page. He stared at the beautiful calligraphy of Robbie's handwriting, tracing the ornate letters with his fingers.

"What are you going to do, Jonathan?"

"Just follow Robbie's instructions." He stepped forward towards the fire and carefully tossed the diary on top of the hot embers. They watched together as the edges darkened and the text on the first page melded into blackness before the diary itself ignited in flames.

ABOUT THE AUTHOR

 SPF Cameron was born in in Red Lake Falls, Minnesota in 1964. He was raised as one of nine children and received his *Juris Doctorate* from the University of Minnesota Law School. He graduated from the University of North Dakota after studying at the University of Oslo in Norway. He has lived and worked in Alaska, New York, Connecticut, Norway, Sweden and England and currently lives in Sevenoaks, England and Kil, Sweden.

ALSO BY SPF CAMERON

Ravens of the Norse

The Old Trapper's Cabin

Catfish Island

In Absentia

The Vincent and Theo Trilogy

CONTACT THE AUTHOR

 You can contact the author by e-mail or follow him on social media at the following addresses and URLs.

Facebook: *@SPFCameron*
Twitter: *@SPFCameron*
E-mail: *SPFCameron@outlook.com*
URLs: *Amazon.com/author/SPFCameron*
SPFCameron.wordpress.com

30911446R00063

Printed in Poland
by Amazon Fulfillment
Poland Sp. z o.o., Wrocław